THE HIPPO-NOT-AMUS

For Jason and Sebastien.
– T.P. and J.P.

To lovely little James, welcome to the world.
– G.P.-R.

Text copyright © 2003 by Tony and Jan Payne
Illustrations copyright © 2003 by Guy Parker-Rees

First published in Great Britain in 2003 by Gullane Children's Books

Library of Congress Cataloging-in-Publication Data available

ISBN 0-439-56418-2

10 9 8 7 6 5 4 3 2 1   04 05 06 07 08

Printed in Hong Kong
Reinforced binding for library use
First Scholastic edition, February 2004

THE HIPPO-NOT-AMUS

By Tony and Jan Payne

Illustrated by Guy Parker-Rees

Orchard Books
An Imprint of Scholastic Inc.
New York

Portly was a very young hippopotamus. He didn't ask to be a hippopotamus — he was just born that way, and he wasn't sure he wanted to be one forever.

Hippos stood up to their eyes in water all day.
They ate boring old grass all day. What sort of
a life was that?

One day, Portly said to his mom and dad, "I've been a hippo for long enough, and now I want to be something else."

"Impossible!" said his dad, shaking his head.

"You're a hippopotamus, and that's the way it is," said his mom.

But Portly was a very stubborn hippo. "We'll see about that!" he said, and stomped off. "It's time for me to be something more interesting and to eat stuff with some taste!" he called back.

Portly had not gone far when he met a herd of animals. More hippos, he thought. But as he got closer, he saw that they had big spikes where their noses should be! You could do a lot of, umm. . . well, tossing stuff around, with spikes like that, he thought.

"Excuse me," Portly said politely to the nearest animal. "What sort of creature are you?"

"I'm a rhinoceros," said the animal through a mouthful of twigs.

"Well, I'm going to be a rhino. . . thingy, too!" said Portly. "But first I need some spikes! Where did you get yours?"

The rhinoceros laughed. "You could say
I got my horns from my mother."
"Does she have any more?" asked Portly.
"No," said the rhino. "You have to grow your own."
"We'll see about that!" said the little hippo.

Portly found two pieces of wood and sharpened them until they were pointed, like horns.

He tied them on his nose, but then he couldn't see.

He tied them to the sides of his head. He tied them on top of his head. He tied them underneath his chin. No matter what, they just didn't look right!

He turned around to ask for some advice, but the rhinos were gone! So Portly continued on his journey with the horns sticking out just anywhere.

Before long, Portly saw a strange animal hanging upside down from a tree. That looked like fun!

"Excuse me," he said. "What sort of creature are you?"

"I'm a bat, I think," said the animal. "And you are...?"

"I'm a hippo... noceros, actually," said Portly. "So what do bats do?"

The bat took ages to
answer.

"Eat stuff. . . hang
out. . . . It's not easy
being a bat," he
added.

"We'll see about
that!" said Portly.

He made some hooks out
of bananas and tied them
to his feet. Carefully, he
climbed into the tree and
then hung upside down.
"Now what?" he asked.
"Now," said the bat, "we wait."
"For what?" Portly wanted to know.

The bat thought hard.
"Wednesday!" he said.
So Portly settled down
to wait for Wednesday.

But after five minutes the bananas slipped, and he fell out of the tree! That's when Portly decided that five minutes was just about the right amount of time to be a bat.

A little later Portly found a water hole. Standing in it was an ENORMOUS animal.

"Excuse me," Portly said. "What sort of creature are you?"

"I am an elephant," said the animal. "What, may I ask, are you?"

"I'm a hippo-bat-onoceros! And I'm going to be an elephant, too!" announced Portly. "I want to spit water out of my nose! I want to smell something when I'm *here*, and my nose is *somewhere else*. So I'll want one of those tube things, and I want some big flappy ears! And. . ."

The elephant had to smile. "Wait a second, young hippo-bat-onoceros. You have to be *born* with those things." But Portly was determined. "We'll see about that!"

Portly made big ears from two large leaves.
Then he made a trunk out of a vine,
but what could he do with it? He wanted
to trumpet tunes and pluck leaves and
spit with it! But he couldn't.

So Portly decided to find something else he could be.

His journey was slow because his horns fell over his eyes.
His hooks caught in bushes.

He kept tripping over his trunk. And
his ears flapped all over the place.

By now Portly was getting a bit
bored with all this excitement.
He kept thinking about water
for some reason.

Portly had not gone far when he met some new animals. They started on the ground, like you and me, but ended up above the trees!

"Excuse me," said Portly to a knobby knee. "What sort of creature are you?"

A head appeared from the leaves.

"I'm a giraffe," it said.

"What do giraffes do?" called the little hippo.

"Eat leaves, mainly!" said the giraffe.

"Can a hippo-ele-bat-onoceros eat leaves?" Portly inquired.

"I should think a hippo-ele-bat-onoceros could eat anything!" replied the giraffe.

"Then I'll be a giraffe!" said Portly.

"But it takes years to grow all the way up here!" exclaimed the giraffe.

"We'll see about that!" said Portly.

Portly made two tall stilts out of branches and strapped them to his legs. But it was hard being so high up.

Portly was now as hot and as hungry as a hippo can be. *I know just what I need!* he thought. And Portly started out on the long trail that led back to the river.

Portly's mom and dad were standing up to their eyes in water when they saw their son.

"Excuse me," said Mom, knowing who it was but not letting on. "What sort of creature are you?"

"I'm a hippo-gir-ele-bat-onoceros!" Portly said proudly.

"Well, are you hungry?" asked his mom kindly. "I'm afraid we only have boring old grass for supper. Do hippo-gir-ele-bat-onoceroses eat boring old grass?"

"As a matter of fact," said Portly, "they like it more than anything."

"Then come and join us!" said Dad.

So the young hippopotamus
removed his stilts and slid
into the river.
The water felt
wonderful,
and the boring
old grass tasted
better than ever. He did
not notice his ears floating away, his trunk
sinking, and his hooks and horns falling off.

Mom smiled at Portly. "Our own little hippo doesn't want to be a hippo anymore, so there's plenty of room for you, if you'd like to stay?"

"Hmmm," said Portly, looking up at some nearby monkeys and wondering what it would be like to swing from tree to tree by his tail. . . .

"We'll see about that!"